This book
belongs to

....

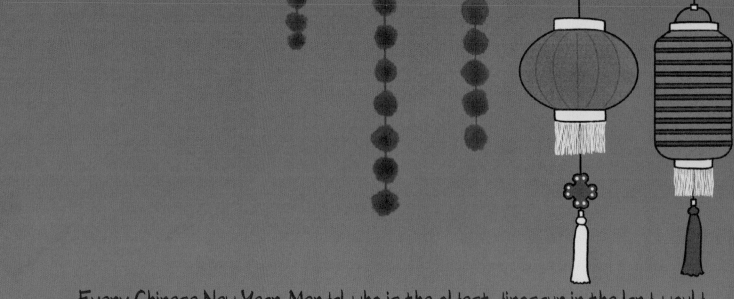

Every Chinese New Year, Mendal, who is the oldest dinosaur in the land, would come down to the forest to celebrate the new year. All the dinosaurs would eat yummy food and enjoy the magical fireworks.

But this year, Mendal was unable to make it down the mountains and into the dinosaur village.

Topsy, Logan and Violet decided they would make the trip to the Red mountain. If Mendal could not make it to the village to celebrate with them, they would bring the celebrations to him.

They all sat down to draw and make cards and gifts for him. Topsy packed his bag with dumplings, spring rolls and glutinous rice cake. Violet put sweet rice balls into her bag; they would eat these during the Lantern Festival. Logan had made some longevity noodles especially for Mendal. He also packed juicy tangerines.

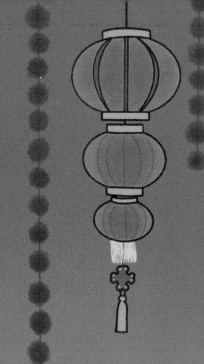

"Don't forget to bring the pomelos. My mom told me the more you eat, the more wealth it will bring!" said Topsy.

And off they went.

Shortly after they had begun their journey, they came across a swamp that had quicksand.

"Oh no, how will we get across?" asked Logan.

"I have a good idea," they heard a tiny voice say.

It was Rat. They knew he could be trusted to come up with a plan and quick; after all, he was known for being quick-witted.

"We need to make some kind of bridge so you can all safely cross. I know, Ox! Ox where are you?" shouted Rat.

Ox heard and came right away. Rat knew he would. After all, Ox was known for being dependable.

"Hello everyone. What's the matter?" Ox said.

"The dinos need help getting across the quicksand," Rat replied. "Do you think you could help by ramming that tree down? Then they can walk across it."

"Of course, I can," Ox said happily.

He immediately started to ram his head into the tree.
With a few strong pushes, the tree began to fall.

Now the dinosaurs could safely walk across the quicksand.

Rabbit had heard them long before they had spotted him. After all, he was known for being alert.

Rabbit and Tiger were racing. They were always racing. Rabbit was super quick, and Tiger loved to race against him. After all, he was known for being competitive.

"Where are you guys going?" asked Tiger.

"To the red mountain to celebrate New Year with Mendal," said Violet.

"You must be thirsty. Here, take this water." Rabbit kindly gave all the dinosaurs a drink.

"Thank you," said the dinosaurs.

"We better get going," said Topsy.

Violet spotted some caves ahead. "Oh no, look over there. It looks kinda scary!" she said, trying not to panic too much.

"I don't want to walk past the caves," said Logan.

"Don't worry. I will go ahead and make sure everything is okay," said Tiger. After all, he was also known for being brave.

Tiger led the dinosaurs past the dark caves. As they walked past, a voice shouted out, "Hey Tiger. Is that you?"

Dragon came out.

"Oh, hey Dragon," they all said.

"We were scared to walk past the caves. We thought there might be a scary creature lurking in them," said Logan.

Dragon laughed. "Nope, just me and Snake! We are busy making lanterns."

Snake and Dragon had made lots or lanterns. Eighty-eight, to be precise.

"Wow, they are amazing!" said Violet.

"Who came up with all the riddles and wrote them on the lanterns?" asked Topsy.

"I came up with the riddles, and Dragon did all the writing," replied Snake.

"Fantastic! After all, Dragon and Snake are known for their intelligence!" exclaimed Tiger.

Dragon gave the dinosaurs eight lanterns to take with them.

The dinosaurs said goodbye to Tiger, Dragon and Snake.

Then they continued on their journey.

It was getting late, and they were starting to get tired.

They had made it to the halfway point, the Yuanyang Rice Terraces.

Horse and Goat were grazing when they noticed the young dinosaurs.

"Topsy, Logan, Violet! Long time no see!" Horse shouted excitedly.

"Hi Horse and Goat," said Violet.

The two friends could see that the dinosaurs needed to rest.

"Why don't you all take a rest this evening? Then you will be nice and fresh in the morning," Goat suggested.

Horse and Goat gave the dinosaurs blankets and shelter. After all, they were both known for being kind.

Bright and early the next morning, Horse woke them up. He was full of energy, as usual. The sun was rising above the rice terraces. It was a magnificent sight.

Before they left, Goat presented them with a beautiful dragon dance costume. She had made it out of grass, bamboo and paper. It was beautiful. After all, Goat was also known for being creative.

Topsy thanked them dearly for their kindness.

Across the fields next to the blue mountain was a large lake. Monkey and Rooster were fishing there. They were catching fish for the holiday feast. Rooster had made the fishing rod from a bamboo stick and vines. After all, he was known for being resourceful like that.

"Hey dinos, would you like to take some fish with you to Mendal? You can't celebrate the new year without fish!" said Rooster.

"Yes please!" said Logan.

"We need to get to the red mountains. Which is the quickest way?" asked Topsy.

"I can take you to the end of the Red River," said Monkey. "Dog and Pig live there. I could use some excitement." After all, Monkey was known for being adventurous.

Monkey eagerly led the dinosaurs while swinging from branch to branch and whistling his favorite song.

He dropped them off where the Red River ended and the Lishe River started. Dog and Pig were busy getting ready for the celebrations.

"Could you help us get to the Red mountain?" Asked Violet.

"Of course, I can," said Dog. "Anything for my dinosaur friends." After all, Dog was known for being loyal. But also cautious. "You have too much stuff to make it across the river. We must pack it in a box in order to travel safely," Dog said.

Pig helped pack all their stuff in a box. Then gave each of the young dinosaurs a red envelope, which had money and gold coins in it. "This is from Mrs. Pig and me." After all, Pig was known for being generous!

"Wow, thank you so much!" said the little dinos.

They hopped on board the boat with their box and Dog and waved farewell to Pig.

It was very windy, and the boat was rocking from side to side. They didn't know if they would make it. Dog thought it was a good idea to turn back. But the dinos insisted that they wanted to make it to the red mountain.

Suddenly, a gust of wind flipped the boat over. The water was icy cold. Violet, Topsy and Dog made it onto dry land.

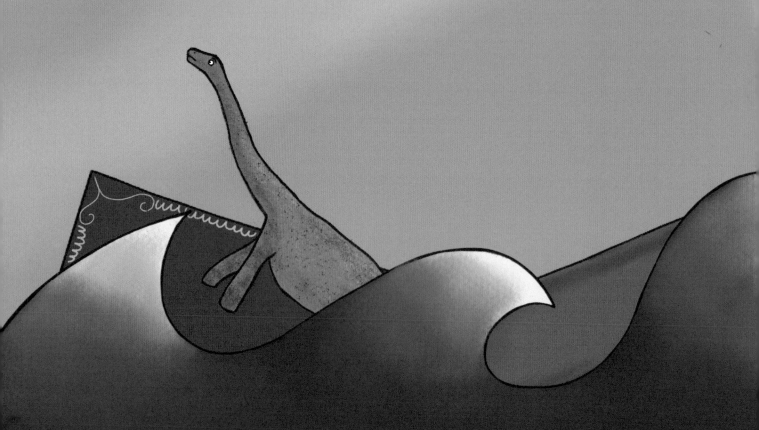

"Oh no! Where is Logan?" said Topsy.

"I can see him. He's floating on top of the box!" Said Dog.

They all let out a sigh of relief.

At last, they made it to the red mountain.

They knocked on Mendal's door. He was shocked to see them but very happy.
"What a wonderful surprise!"

"We did make you gifts and cards, but they got ruined," said Logan.

"The boat tipped over," added Topsy.

"As long as you are all okay, then it doesn't matter. Having you here is the best gift I could receive," replied Mendal.

"Luckily, we have our box of goodies! Thanks to Dog!" Said Logan.

They unpacked the box and prepared the feast. Finally, they were all ready to celebrate Chinese New Year.

Except for Dog...he was already fast asleep.

If you have enjoyed this book, I kindly ask
you to leave a review on Amazon. It makes
a huge difference for independent
Authors and Artists like myself.

Thank you so much!

Jessica